This book belong

Pronunciation Guide

Awaat Pauni: Aa-waat Pau-nee

Bhangra: Bhung-raa

Birjeet: Beer-jeet

Chacha: Chaa-chaa

Chachi: Chaa-Chee

Chintu: Cheen-too

Chunni: Choon-nee

Dhol: Dhol

Gehun: Gay-hoon

Kara: Kuh-da

Khunda: Khoon-Daa

Kirpan: Keer-paan

Kurta: Koor-taa

Langar: Lung-gurh

Lassi: Luss-ee

Nanak: Naa-Nuk

Pugdee: Pug-dee

Punjab: Pun-jaab

Roti: Row-tee

Salwaar: Sul-waar

Sarson: Sir-soan

Sat Sri Akaal: Sut-Sree-Akaal

Sikh: Seekh

Simran: Seem-run

Tamba: Tum-baa

Tumbi: Toom-bee

Vaisakhi: Vai-saa-khee

Note for parents: Our books provide a glimpse into the beautiful cultural diversity of India, including occasional mythology references.

Printed in the United States of America. First Edition.

's India Adventure Series, Book 7

Let's Celebrate Vaisakhi!

Harvest Festival of Punjab

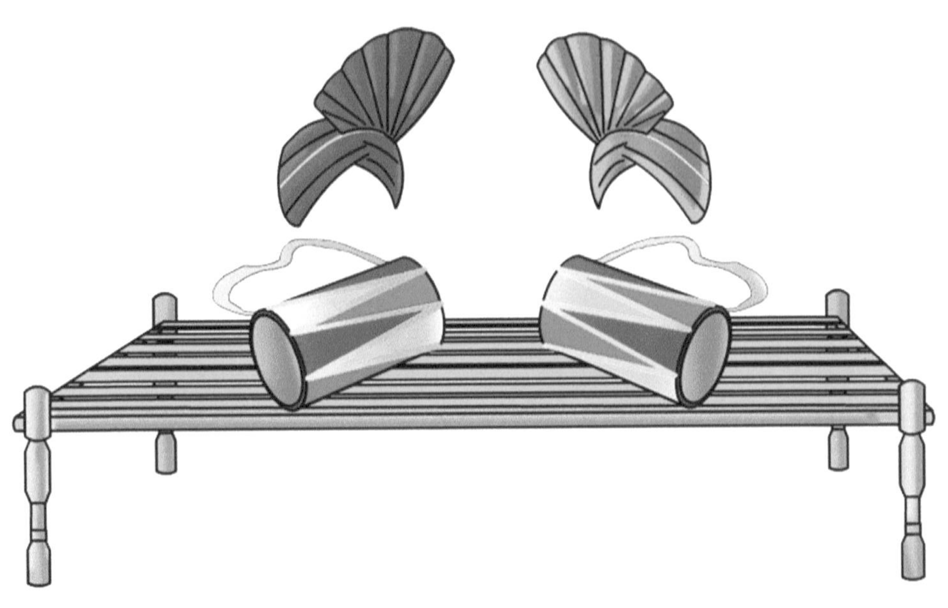

Written by:
Ajanta & Vivek

Hi! I'm Maya. I love to go on fun adventures in India with my brother, Neel.
Hi! I'm Neel. We live in Chicago. We just landed in Punjab to celebrate Vaisakhi! Come join us.
Hi! I am Chintu, the squirrel. I love to join my friends on their trips.

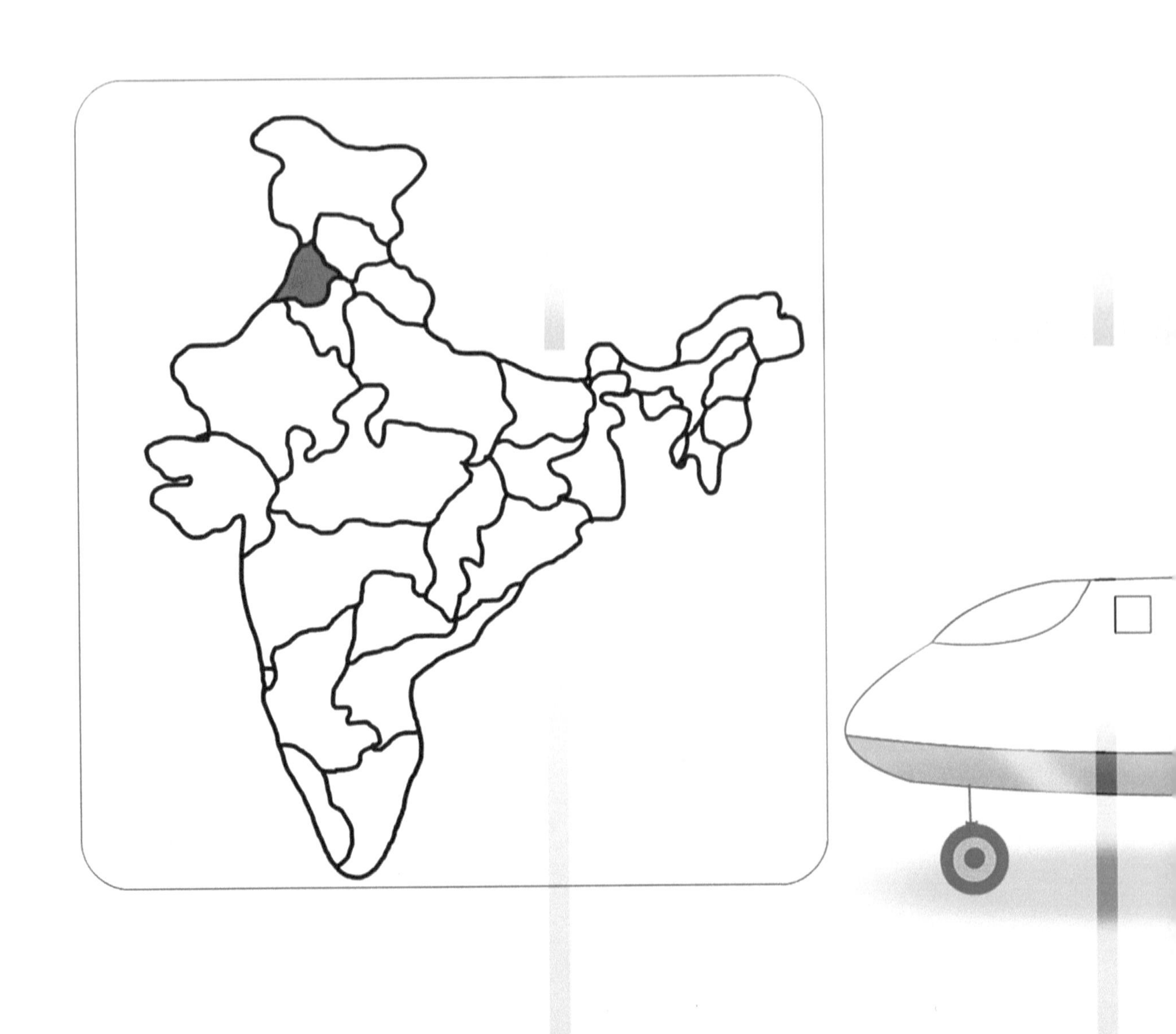

This is a map of India. India is a big country. It has many states, languages, festivals, and dances.

Do you see the red spot on the map? That is the state of Punjab.

Vaisakhi is the harvest festival of Punjab.

Maya and Neel arrive at their uncle Birjeet's farm.

In India, Dad's brother is called *Chacha*. *Chacha* greets them with a big smile "*Sat Sri Akaal* kids".

"What does that mean, Birjeet *Chacha*?" the kids ask. "That is how we greet in Punjab" explains *Chacha*.

"*Sat Sri Akaal Chacha*", say Maya, Neel and Chintu.

Neel hesitates a bit and then asks slowly "*Chacha,* do you always wear your turban?".

"I am so glad you asked, Neel. I am a Sikh and that's why I wear a turban. Hop on the cart and I can tell you more." *Chacha* replies.

INFO ZOOM

Who are the Sikh?

Birjeet *Chacha* is a Sikh. Who are the Sikh?

Sikhs are originally from a place called Punjab in India. They have 10 Gurus or teachers.

Sikhs believe in being kind and loving to all.

Guru Nanak was the first teacher. He travelled for 30 years to teach people about love and peace.

He also started *Langar*. *Langar* is a free kitchen. Many, many people can eat together for free at a *Langar*.

Langar also helps poor people who do not have enough to eat.

Sikhs keep long hair. They tie their long hair with a turban on their head. Just like *Chacha*.

They also wear a bracelet called *Kara*. The *Kara* reminds them to do good with their hands.

Some also carry a small knife called *Kirpan*. The *Kirpan* reminds them to protect those in need.

Chacha drives the cart through the farm.

"What are you growing here, *Chacha*?" Neel asks.

Chacha points to the right "Do you see the one with yellow flowers? That is Mustard or *Sarson*."

Pointing to the left he says "This is Wheat or *Gehun*. Punjab is famous for growing both."

"What do you do when the plant is all grown up?" Maya wonders. "Aha" exclaims *Chacha* "That's when we harvest. Let me tell you about it."

INFO ZOOM

Steps of Farming

First, we have to make the dirt soft. Some people in India use a plow. Two strong bulls pull the plow together and get the farm ready.

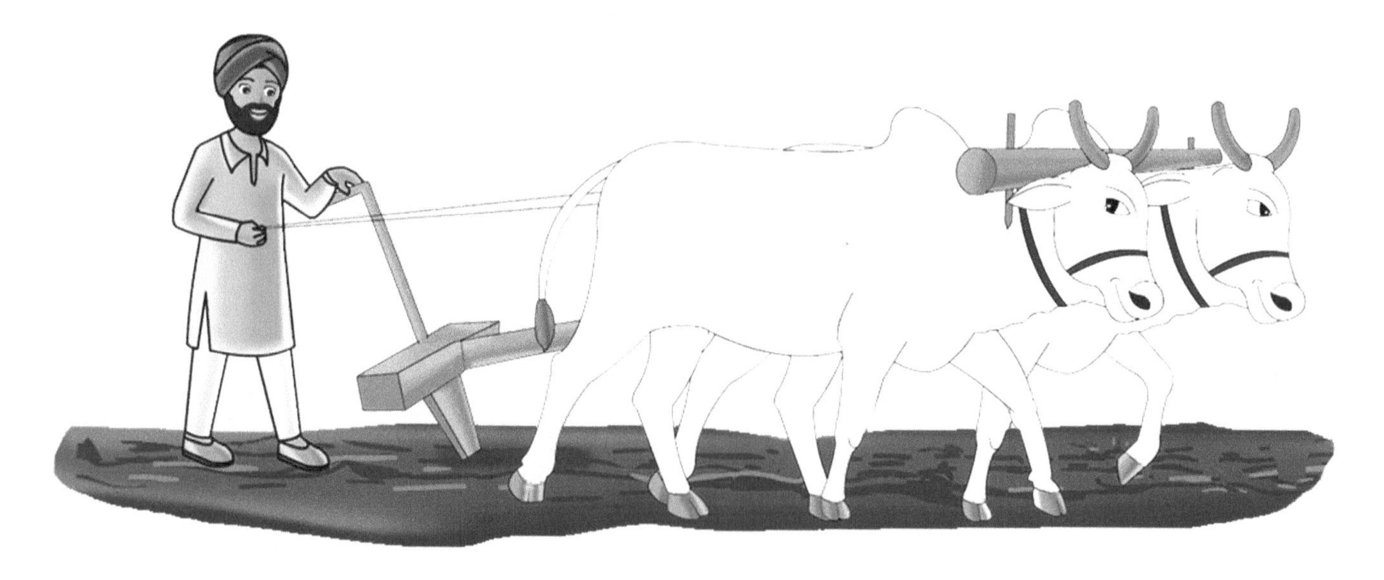

Then we put the seeds in the soft dirt. This is called planting.

Next, we water the seeds and baby plants pop their little heads out.

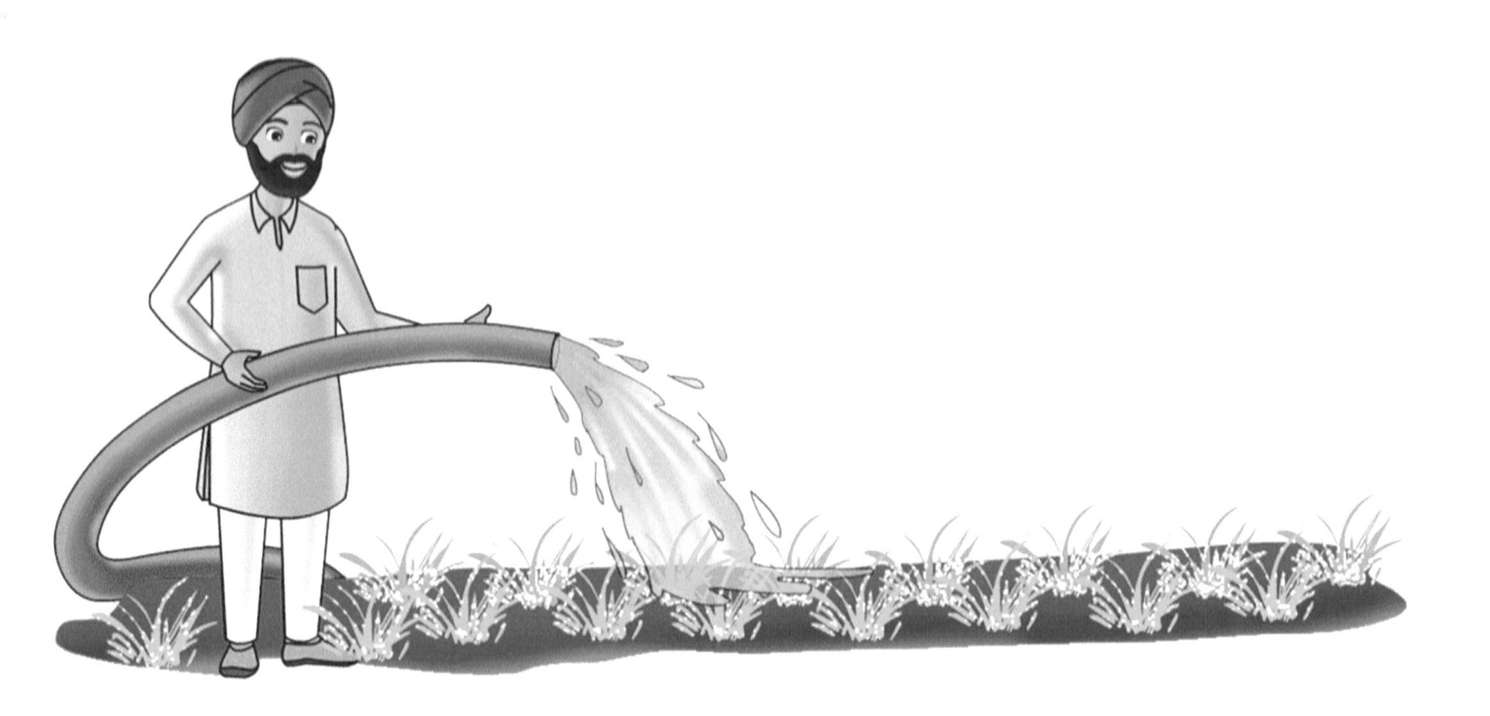

Once the plants are all grown up, we pick them to cook and eat or sell in the market. This picking is called harvesting.

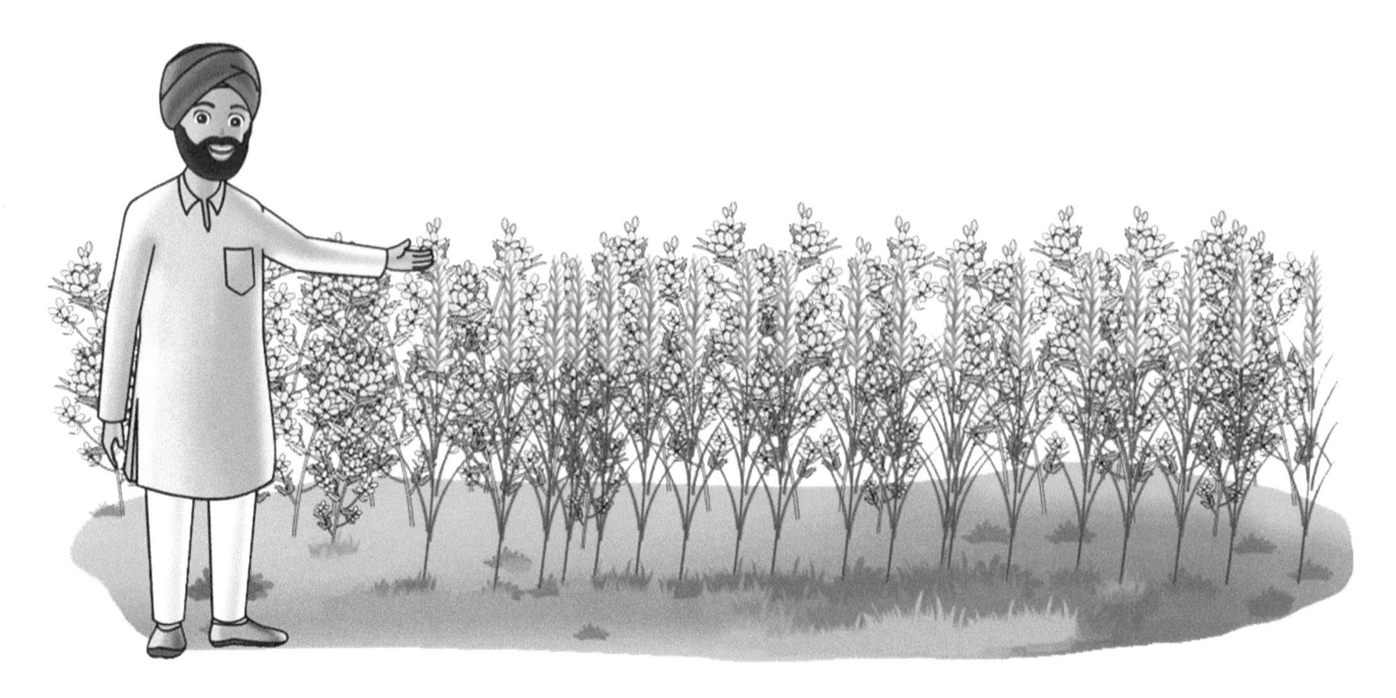

Harvest time is a very happy time. In Punjab, we celebrate harvest-time with a festival called *Vaisakhi*.

Walking along, the kids hear voices singing beautiful songs.

"Who is singing, *Chacha*?" the kids ask.

"Those are farmers harvesting together in a big group. This fun group activity is called *Awaat Pauni*".

Maya, Neel and Chintu eagerly jump up in the air “Can we help too?”.

“Of course, let’s join them!” *Chacha* says with a laugh.

They all join in. Neel helps by taking *Gehun* off the plants. Maya carries the plucked Sarson in a basket on her head.

Suddenly, they hear drum beats. "Hooray, the *Dhol* players are here!" *Chacha* says, "The *Dhol* music makes harvesting even more fun".

Everyone works together for hours. It is so much fun, singing and working.

At lunch time, *Chacha* calls Maya and Neel "You have worked very hard today. Let's take a break and eat".

Everyone sits together for a picnic.

"Neel, can you please pass me the *Roti*" *Chacha* asks. Neel looks around. "What is *Roti*?" he wonders. *Chacha* picks up the round bread "This is called *Roti* and is made from *Gehun*".

Maya eats a spoonful of the green curry from a bowl "And what is this yummy curry?" Maya asks. "It is called *Saag*. It is made from leaves of *Sarson* plant" *Chacha* explains.

"Sluuuuurrpp" Chintu sips a white milky drink loudly. Everyone laughs.

"Looks like you love *Lassi,* Chintu. *Lassi* is like milkshake and is very refreshing in hot weather" Chacha says with a smile.

After lunch, *Chacha* gets the cart ready. "Your auntie, Simran *Chachi,* is home and has a surprise for you." *Chacha* says. "Oh, how exciting! Let's go home." the kids exclaim.

"We are home" *Chacha* announces.

He helps everyone get off and then gives food and water to the bulls.

Simran *Chachi* meets the kids and gives them warm hugs.

"*Sat Sri Akaal* kids. I am so happy you are here to celebrate *Vaisakhi* with us. Come inside and check out your surprise".

The kids can barely wait and rush inside.

Inside the house, Maya and Neel find beautiful new clothes waiting for them. The kids try them on right away.

Chachi explains to Maya "*Your* shirt is called *Kurta* and your pants are called *Salwar*. This beautiful cloth on top is called a *Chunni*."

Chacha tells Neel "Your shirt is called *Kurta* too but your pants are called *Tamba*. The turban on your head with a big fan is called a *Pugdee*.

Chacha then puts a tiny *Pugdee* on Chintu's head. "Oh WOW! I get to dress up too!" Chintu squeals with joy.

The kids hear the sound of the *Dhol* again. They rush out to the street.

They see lots and lots of people walking, dancing, singing and playing the *Dhol*.

"What's happening, *Chachi?*" Maya asks.

"This is the *Vaisakhi* procession or parade where everyone in the village walks together.

The dancers in the front are dancing *Bhangra*." Chachi explains.

INFO ZOOM

What is Bhangra?

People of Punjab dance *Bhangra* during *Vaisakhi*. It is a dance to celebrate harvest-time.

Some of the dance moves come from what people do everyday. For example, farmers usually carry a big stick with them in the farm.

When they dance *Bhangra*, they sometimes use a stick too.

Bhangra dancers do lots of cool stunts with spins and lifts. This dance makes you strong!

Bhangra music uses a lot of fun instruments such as *Tumbi* (like guitar) and *Dhol* (like drums).

Bhangra dance uses a lot of fun props like *Saap* (because it looks like a snake) and *Khunda* (a stick with a curved end).

“This looks like so much fun! Can we join?”, the kids ask.

“Of course. This is a time for everyone to celebrate together”, *Chacha* says with a smile.

Chachi, kids and Chintu join in the fun procession dancing and singing along with everyone.

Chacha also picks up a *Dhol* and plays along.

After a lot of dancing, the procession arrives at the center of the village. Everybody continues to sing, dance and play together.

As the sun sets, everyone relaxes and takes a break.

"We had such a great time exploring Punjab and learning about it!" Maya says.

"Yes, Punjab is an awesome place. From farming, food and music to dance, everything was so much fun!" Neel agrees.

"We cannot wait for our next adventure and wonder where that will be. We hope you can join us then!" say Maya, Neel, and Chintu.

"Until then, *Sat Sri Akaal*!"

INFO RECAP

Let's look back on our wonderful Vaisakhi Celebration...

How do you greet in Punjab?
(Sat Sri Akaal)

Who was the first Sikh teacher?
(Guru Nanak)

What is *Awaat Pauni?*
(Harvesting in a big group)

What are drums from Punjab called? (*Dhol*)

What is Chintu's favorite milkshake from Punjab is called? (*Lassi*)

What clothes of Punjab did Maya wear?
(Kurta, Salwaar & Chunni)

What is Punjab famous for growing? *(Gehun or Wheat & Sarson or Mustard)*

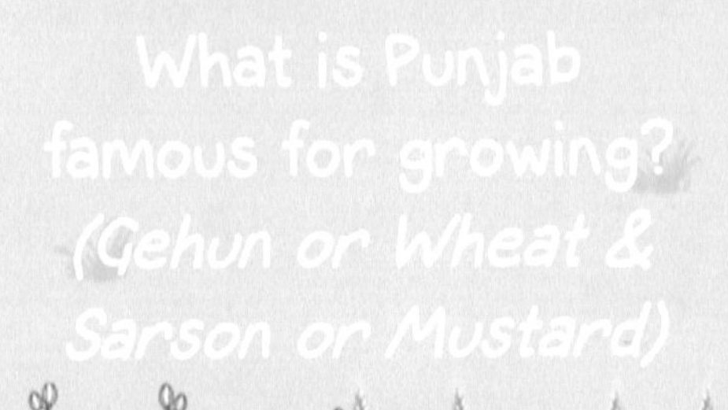

What is *Vaisakhi? (Harvest festival of Punjab)*

What is the mustard curry called? *(Saag)*

What round bread did we eat? *(Roti)*

What clothes of Punjab did Neel wear? *(Kurta, Tamba & Pugdee)*

What is the famous dance from Punjab called? *(Bhangra)*

About the Authors

Ajanta Chakraborty was born in Bhopal, India, and moved to North America in 2001. She earned an MS in Computer Science from the University of British Columbia and also earned a Senior Diploma in Bharatanatyam, a classical Indian dance, to feed her spirit.

Ajanta quit her corporate consulting job in 2011 and took the plunge to run Bollywood Groove (and also Culture Groove) full-time. The best part of her work day includes grooving with classes of children as they leap and swing and twirl to a Bollywood beat.

Vivek Kumar was born in Mumbai, India, and moved to the US in 1998. Vivek has an MS in Electrical Engineering from The University of Texas, Austin, and an MBA from the Kellogg School of Management, Northwestern University.

Vivek has a very serious day job in management consulting. But he'd love to spend his days leaping and swinging, too.

We have been featured on:

We are independent authors who want to help **Raise Multicultural Kids**! We rely on your support to sustain our work:

- ✓ Drop us an Amazon review at: **CultureGroove.com/books**
- ✓ **Share our books as Gifts & Party Favors** (bulk order discounts)
- ✓ Schedule our unique **'Dancing Bookworms' Virtual Author Visits**
- ✓ Join our **FREE** Monthly Stories & Dances workshops: **CultureGroove.com/FREE**

Many thanks!

Culture Groove
Raise Multicultural Kids

CPSIA information can be obtained
at www.ICGtesting.com
Printed in the USA
LVHW071925280422
717159LV00034B/450

* 9 7 8 1 9 4 5 7 9 2 3 5 9 *